Wings

A Tale of Two Chickens

James Marshall

Happy Cat
BOOKS

For
Muriel Korn

Published by
Happy Cat Books
An imprint of Catnip Publishing Ltd
14 Greville Street
London EC1N 8SB

This edition first published 2008
1 3 5 7 9 10 8 6 4 2

Text and illustrations copyright © 1986 by James Marshall
All rights reserved
First published in USA in 1986 by Viking Penguin
under the title WINGS: A TALE OF TWO CHICKENS.
British publication rights arranged by Sheldon Fogelman Agency, Inc.

The moral right of the author/ illustrator has been asserted

A CIP catalogue record for this book is available from the British Library

ISBN 978-1-905117-82-6

Printed in China

www.catnippublishing.co.uk

Harriet and Winnie were as different as two chickens could possibly be.

Harriet was enormously fond of reading.

"Frankly, I'd rather swat flies," said Winnie.

Many interesting hobbies kept Harriet busy all day.

"I'm so bored I could just die," said Winnie.

One afternoon, Winnie was wandering in the garden.
"Nothing really wild ever happens around here," she said.
"Good afternoon," said a silky voice.
But there was no one there.

"Look up!" said the voice.

"My, my," said Winnie.

"Care to go for a spin?" said the stranger.
"Oh, I couldn't," said Winnie.
"Oh, come on," said the stranger. "Live a little."

"Why not?" said Winnie.
And she climbed up the ladder and into the basket.
"Blast off!" cried the stranger.
"Stop! Stop!" cried Harriet.

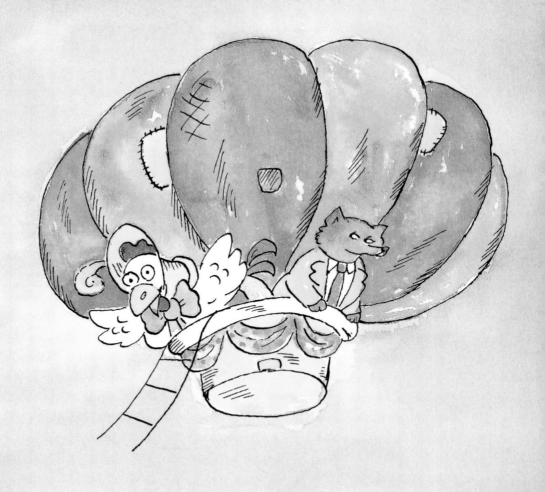

But it was too late.
"I'll be back for dinner!" shouted Winnie.
And they were gone.

"She never did have a lick of sense," said the neighbours.

"Didn't she *know* it was a fox?"
"She never reads," said Harriet.

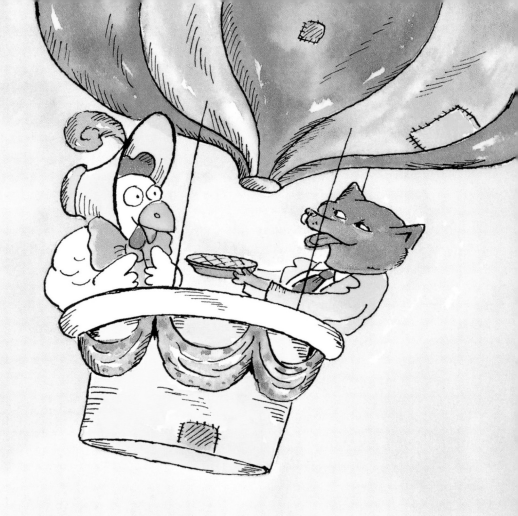

The stranger introduced himself as Mr. Johnson.
"Have a raspberry tart," he said.
"I don't want to get too **plump**," said Winnie.
"**Plump** is nice," said Mr. Johnson.

Harriet went to the cops.

"We'll do our best," said the officer, "but foxes *are* clever."

"We'll see about that," said Harriet.

Mr. Johnson made an unscheduled stop.
"I'll be right back," he said, rushing into a grocery store.
"Quick!" he told the grocer.
"I need a package of instant dumplings!"

Winnie decided to make herself more comfortable.
"I'll just get rid of these useless old sandbags," she said.

Mr. Johnson came out just in time
to see the balloon heading south.

But Winnie was soon bored.
And she left the balloon
at the nearest water tower.
"I'll ask folks around here
how to get home," she said.

Meanwhile, Mr. Johnson hadn't given up hope
of a chicken dinner.
"**A** chicken costume?" said the clerk in the costume store.

"You heard me," said **Mr. Johnson.**

So, wearing his clever new disguise, he went to a place where chickens were known to cross the road.
"Hee-hee," he said. "They'll think I'm one of them."

"Yoo-hoo," said a voice.

Mr. Johnson couldn't believe his luck.
"Is this where chickens cross over?" said Winnie.
"Indeed it is," said Mr. Johnson.

"Travel makes me *so* hungry," said Winnie.

"Care for some sardines?" said Mr. Johnson,
opening his big burlap bag.
"Oooh," said Winnie. "I *love* sardines."

"In you go!" said Mr. Johnson.

"If at first you don't succeed . . ." said Mr. Johnson.
But he soon found the bag was quite heavy.

Just then he heard the sound of bicycle tyres on dry leaves.

"May I be of some assistance?" said a **plump** grey fox.

"I'd be ever so grateful," said Mr. Johnson.

They loaded the bag onto the bicycle and rode away.

"What is in the bag?" asked the **plump** grey fox.
"My laundry," said Mr. Johnson.

At Three Corners it began to rain.
Nothing worse than plucking soggy feathers, thought Mr. Johnson.
"Shall we take shelter at this church?" he suggested.

Inside, the preacher was talking about charity.
"It is our duty to help the needy," he said.

"Humpf," muttered Mr. Johnson.

"And what have we here?" said the preacher.
"Two kind souls have brought a bag of food
to share with the poor."

"No! No!" cried Mr. Johnson.
"Be generous!" cried the preacher.
And the bag ripped open.

"I didn't see any sardines," said Winnie.
"What's this?" cried the preacher.

"Chicken stealing is wicked!"
Mr. Johnson tore out of the church.

The plump grey fox took Winnie by the wing,
and they slipped out of the back door.

"Are we playing a game?" said Winnie.
"Just run!" said the fox.

Soon they found themselves at the edge of a steep cliff.
"Phooey!" said the plump grey fox. "We'll have to turn back."

"Oh, lookee," said Winnie. "Here comes nice Mr. Johnson."
And Mr. Johnson was almost upon them.

"Unhand that chicken!" he cried. "She's mine!"

At that moment, Mr. Johnson's balloon floated by.
The plump grey fox threw Winnie into the basket,
jumped in after her,

and they were gone.
Mr. Johnson was downright furious.

"You have caused me a lot of trouble,"
said the **plump** grey fox.
"Now help me out of this embarrassing costume!"

Winnie was so surprised, she nearly fell out of the balloon.
"Harriet!" she cried. *"You!"*

That evening Harriet put Winnie to bed with a good book.
"Oh, my stars!" cried Winnie. "Mr. Johnson was a *fox!*"
And she nearly died of fright.

"Maybe there's hope for her yet," said Harriet.